Hello Kitty
and friends

The Big Bake Off
·A HELLO KITTY ADVENTURE·

MEET

Hello Kitty

and friends

Hello Kitty

Mimmy

Tammy

Mama

Papa

Grandpa

Grandma

Fifi

Dear Daniel

With special thanks to
Linda Chapman and Michelle Misra

First published in Great Britain by HarperCollins Children's Books in 2015

www.harpercollins.co.uk
1 3 5 7 9 10 8 6 4 2

ISBN: 978-0-00-754072-3

Printed and bound in England by Clays Ltd, St Ives plc.

MIX
Paper from
responsible sources
FSC® C007454

FSC™ is a non-profit international organisation established to promote
the responsible management of the world's forests. Products carrying the
FSC label are independently certified to assure consumers that they come
from forests that are managed to meet the social, economic and
ecological needs of present and future generations,
and other controlled sources.

Find out more about HarperCollins and the environment at
www.harpercollins.co.uk/green

Contents

1. Strawberries Galore!....................9

2. Happy Baking............................25

3. Festival Fun..............................40

4. A New Friend............................53

5. Bake Off Time!..........................68

6. Star Bakers!..............................83

Strawberries Galore!

Hello Kitty stood up and looked down the

long row of strawberry plants. She was picking

fruit with her twin sister Mimmy and their Mama,

at Cherry Tree Farm. It was thirsty work in the

hot sun. Mimmy and Hello Kitty's baskets were

almost full now, although Hello Kitty thought she
had probably eaten as many strawberries as she
had picked! Her pink-and-white polka-dot T-shirt
was decorated with bright red strawberry stains.

Whoops! But she just hadn't been able to resist all the delicious fruit – strawberries, blueberries and raspberries. *Yummy!*

CHERRY TREE
FARM

Hello Kitty *and friends*

Hello Kitty *sighed*

happily. What a totally
SUPER day they were
having. She loved
picking fruit and to
make the day perfect,
her friends were
coming over to Hello

Kitty's house that afternoon

– as soon as she was back from the farm. Hello

Kitty felt a **warm** glow as she thought about

Tammy, Fifi and Dear Daniel. Together they made

up the Friendship Club. They met after school

and in the holidays to do all sorts of fun things

– like crafting and painting, having clothes swaps and sleepovers. Today, however, they were simply meeting up at Hello Kitty's house to play – it was just **too** hot for much else!

Mama White told Hello Kitty and Mimmy that it was time to go and pay for the fruit they had picked. Hello Kitty was a bit embarrassed when the lady at the counter saw all the strawberry stains on her T-shirt but the lady just smiled at her. They always expected the pickers to have some of the strawberries as they gathered their fruit, she said. They wouldn't miss a few more.

Phew!

The lady weighed the boxes of strawberries, and then she moved on to the raspberries and after that the blueberries. Hello Kitty didn't know how much there was but it looked like a lot of fruit! They would be able to make delicious

jams and tarts, and best of all

have big bowls of strawberries

and raspberries with

dollops of fresh

whipped cream on top,

too.

As Hello Kitty stood next to Mama,

waiting for her to pay, she looked around

at the tiny shop. All of a sudden, her eyes were

drawn to some little terracotta flowerpots by

the till. They were very cute – small and pretty –

with little white daisies painted all over them.

Mama White laughed as she noticed Hello Kitty looking at them. They matched Hello Kitty's duvet cover, didn't they? Hello Kitty nodded. She thought they would look so sweet in her room, so she shyly asked Mama if she could buy them.

Pleeaassee?

Mama White smiled again and answered of course she could – but Hello Kitty would have to use her own pocket money. Hello Kitty

nodded quickly and opened her purse; she had just enough for three little pots. She paid

and slid the flowerpots into the back of her pink butterfly backpack. They were quite small so they weren't **too** heavy. Mama White had already paid for their fruit, so she and Mimmy led the way back to the car.

It didn't take them long to drive back to their house and when they got there, they found the rest of the Friendship Club already waiting on the doorstep. They were *early!* Hello Kitty waved to her friends as Mama parked

the car, and as soon as she could she jumped out and they all piled into the house. Tammy was holding a leaflet and looking very excited... She had already told the others what it was all about, but she couldn't *wait* to tell Hello Kitty and Mimmy!

Hello Kitty read the leaflet. **Wow!** There was going to be a food festival happening that very weekend in their local park. It had been set up to celebrate yummy food and there were going to be loads of activities for both adults and children. **Best** of all, there was going to be a baking workshop where they could go to make  pizzas and sandwiches and biscuits for the picnic at the end of the day! The picnic would be held in a big garden tent. All the children baking would also be allowed to make their very own *cake*, and even better, there would be a prize for the most original one! Fifi burst in – all of the other parents had already agreed that they could enter. Could Hello Kitty and Mimmy come and bake a cake too?

Just at that moment Mama White came into the room with a big jug of home-made lemonade and some cups. She set them down and looked at the leaflet. She agreed it really did look **brilliant**, but not just because of the cooking and baking workshop. There was a bread trail too; cheese stands; and she was sure

that Papa White might like to try out the cider

pressing. Of course Hello Kitty and Mimmy could

go – they all would! The Friendship Club all

looked at each other and cheered.

Hooray!

Mama White smiled and pointed out that they would all have to get in some cake-making practice, though, if they wanted to enter the cake competition. There would be some *very* good bakers there.

Everyone nodded their heads eagerly. It sounded like the best day ever!

Mama White gave the leaflet back to Tammy and said she would go and fetch them all some **big** bowls of strawberries and cream!

The others cheered again but Hello Kitty let out a loud groan. As delicious as strawberries were, she thought she *might* have had enough for one day!

Happy Baking

Hello Kitty hummed happily to herself. It was

the very next day and already she was hard at

work baking! Grandma White had come over

to help her while Mama and Mimmy had gone

out to do the grocery shopping. Hello Kitty had

already made a batch of heart-shaped cookies

for when the Friendship Club came over later,

but now she wanted to bake

something else. Hmmmm....

Maybe she should practise

her cake for the

competition?

Hello Kitty

turned to her

grandma. What

sort of cake did

Grandma White think that Hello

Kitty should bake for the competition?

She needed something really original. Did

Grandma have any ideas? Grandma White

smiled and shook her head. She had a few

ideas but if it was a competition for an original

cake then it was important that Hello Kitty came

up with her own.

Hello Kitty and friends

Hello Kitty **sighed**

and nodded. She knew

that Grandma White

was right, but what

was she going to

do? Perhaps one

of Mama's cookery

books would help

her to come up with

something. She started flicking through the

pages – lemon sponge cake, chocolate fudge

cake, carrot cake – they were all *delicious*, of

course, but none of them were new. Hello Kitty

came to one of her favourites – white chocolate

and raspberry cake. It really was yummy, but…

Maybe she should just forget about the

competition for now and make that for

her friends. After all, they had lots of

raspberries they needed to use up, and

her friends really did **love** it!

Hello Kitty started measuring

out the flour and butter, then she

weighed the raspberries

that they'd bought

at the fruit farm. Finally, she got

Grandma White to chop the white

chocolate. Now all that was needed

was the eggs, sugar and flour. Once she had put

them in, she gave all of the ingredients a good

stir and poured them into the tin so Grandma

could put it in the oven.

It would only need to bake for twenty to twenty-five minutes – just until it was golden brown – and in the meantime, she had the biscuits she'd made earlier to ice!

The Friendship Club usually brought their membership cards to each of the meetings and put them in the *middle* of the table; it always made their meetings feel more grown up! This time though, Hello Kitty wanted to set out each of her friends' places with their own cookie, with their name on them in icing. She picked up the icing pen and started to pipe their names

on to the cookies in their **favourite** colours

– purple for Fifi, blue for Tammy,\ red for Dear

Daniel. And pink for herself, of course.

She had just finished when the buzzer went off

on the oven. The cake was **ready!** Grandma

White opened the oven door and they peered

inside to see a lovely round honey-yellow cake with splodges of raspberries in it. Grandma White took it **out** of the oven and set it on the side to cool. And just in the nick of time as well as, at that very moment, the front door bell rang!

Hello Kitty went to answer it and all of
her friends spilled in *excitedly.* They really
wanted to talk about their
ideas for their cakes!
Dear Daniel was
going to do a
giant spider cake.
He would ice it
all over with

chocolate icing and
use liquorice for the
legs and orange and green
jelly drops for the feet and eyes. Fifi was going
to make cupcakes with an ice-skating theme. She

LOVED ice-skating! She had decided
she would ice some cupcakes with
white icing so they looked like
mini ice rinks and then **decorate**
each of them with little plastic
model skaters. Tammy was going
to make a bookworm cake – that was

a bit of a joke as Tammy

L♥VED books. It was

going to be a sponge

cake, made to look like

a book with a yellow

worm in a top hat

coming out of the cover.

And what about Hello Kitty? What was she going to do?

Hello Kitty admitted that while she'd been **thinking** hard, she hadn't come up with anything yet. And she'd been too busy baking

the biscuits and the chocolate and raspberry cake!

Grandma White appeared at that moment with the fresh cake on a plate, covered in white

icing and decorated with fresh

raspberries.

Ta da! All of

the Friendship Club

agreed that it looked

completely delicious.

They were very glad Hello

Kitty and Grandma had spent the morning

making it! As they tucked

into big slices, Fifi

mumbled that

it was so yummy,

Hello Kitty should

bake it as a cake

for the competition. Tammy **giggled** – Fifi

shouldn't talk with her mouth so full!

Hello Kitty wasn't sure

though. How could

a plain cake be

enough when all

of her friends

had come up with

such imaginative

ideas? She would try and

think up something else. After all, there was still

plenty of time. A good idea would come to her

soon. But for now, it was time for the special

cookies. Everyone **squealed** and thanked

Hello Kitty, who blushed and smiled. If only she could make the cookies for the competition – oh well!

Festival Fun!

Three days later Hello Kitty **still** hadn't

come up with an idea for a cake that she wanted

to bake for the competition. The trouble was

that she just didn't have time to think – the

holidays were so busy! She and Mimmy had

been at tennis camp every afternoon. They had visited Waterworld one morning and been out with Grandma White another morning. *Now*, here they were, on the day of the Food Festival and she still didn't know what she was going to do! She would *have* to bake the raspberry and white chocolate cake after all.

Hello Kitty sighed. She felt a little bit disappointed with herself for not coming up with something more original, but she was determined not to let that spoil the festival – the sun was shining and she was about to spend the day with her friends. The park looked totally **AMAZING!** There was brightly coloured bunting hanging from tree to tree and small colourful little umbrellas shading the outside tables. The tables themselves were filled with the most amazing array of foods – from jams to cheeses to pastries to juices – so many trays packed with the most incredible selection of goodies! There was a bouncy castle as well, and balloons marking

each of the entrance points to the park. In the middle of it all stood the **biggest** tent you had ever seen. It was open on two sides so that it was light and airy inside.

Hello Kitty and Mimmy waited with Mama and Papa near the entrance. They had arranged to meet the rest of the Friendship Club and their parents there. Hello Kitty adjusted her backpack.

She had grabbed it that morning to carry her

cardigan, notebook, pen and purse but she'd

forgotten to take the plant pots out and

with all the other things, it was a little bit heavy.

Just then, Dear Daniel appeared and gave

Hello Kitty a little wave. His dad was there

too and he had his camera strapped over his

shoulder. He was going to be taking **lots** of

snapshots of the day, so they would

have lots of nice photos to

remember it with!

And now here were

the others. Tammy was

skipping along with her twin

brother, Timmy. Her parents

were following on behind, and

behind her was Fifi, coming

with her parents too.

All of the parents

greeted each other

and then they paid their

entrance fees and made their way into the park.

There was plenty of time to look around before

the baking and cooking workshop started! There

were so many people there it was hard to walk

around in a big group so they all agreed to meet

at the big tent later and then they split up.

Hello Kitty set off with

her parents and Mimmy.

She wanted to do

some food tasting

and some apple

b⁰bbing, but

she also wanted to sit

down for a little bit with

her notebook and see if she could come up with

a last-minute cake idea! Mama White wanted

to check out the cheese stand and Mimmy was

going to try chocolate tasting. Papa White said

that he would take her there – would Hello Kitty

like to do that, too? But Hello Kitty shook

her head. She really did want to just sit down

and try to think of cake ideas.

Mama and Papa White said that she could

do that – as long as she sat under the shade of

the trees **near** the cheese stand where Mama

could keep an eye on her!

Hello Kitty agreed that she wouldn't move from the spot. Then she **plonked** herself down on the grass, and pulled off her backpack. She took out her notebook and started to think hard…

For five minutes she sat, chewing on her pencil and *trying* to think, but there were so many

things to look at around her that she kept getting distracted and her notebook remained empty. Suddenly, she heard a strange noise.

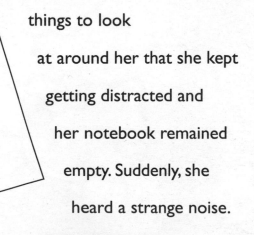

She looked all round but couldn't see anything.

Was it her imagination, or had she just heard

a little whimper? There it was again! A definite

little *whine* coming from the trees behind her.

It sounded like an animal… WHAT could it be?

A New Friend

Hello Kitty got up and started peering around the trees. She gasped when she saw two little dark eyes looking at her anxiously from the shadows. It was a puppy with a chocolate-brown coat and darker brown

markings! He was very small and very cute. But he looked scared. He couldn't be more than a few months old – he was wearing a smart red collar that had a lead trailing from the end of it.

Poor little thing! He must have lost his owner. Hello Kitty walked slowly towards him but the little puppy backed away. Hello Kitty stopped and thought hard. She didn't want him to run off. If only she could get the lead, she could catch him. But *how* could she do that when she couldn't get close enough? If only she had some treats in her bag but all she had was her pen, notebook, cardigan and the little flowerpots.

Hmmm... Maybe they would work.

She knew puppies were usually very curious! He might want to see what they were...

She took the flowerpots and some pens out of her bag and scattered them on the ground, then she knelt down beside them and held still.

The puppy looked puzzled – still a little bit nervous, but definitely interested.

56

He sniffed the air, and took one step forward. Hello Kitty *murmured* encouragement to him under her breath and put her hand out gently. He started moving forward, his nose twitching curiously. One step… two steps… until finally he reached the pots and pens and started *sniffing* them. Hello Kitty reached out and took hold of his

lead. He started sniffing her hand, and then
climbed on to her knee and licked her face as if
he was saying he wanted to be her friend! She
stroked him. He was SO cute. His owner must
be really missing him.

She picked him
up and looked
around. What
should she do
now? She didn't
want to leave
the trees after
she'd **promised**

Mama she would stay

there. Hopefully she would come back soon and

know what to do. But just then, Hello Kitty saw

one of the festival helpers walking by. The lady

was wearing the festival's uniform of a blue and

yellow polo shirt and she was selling information

programmes to people. Hello Kitty called out to her and the lady came over. Was Hello Kitty OK? Was she lost? Hello Kitty held up the puppy. She wasn't lost — but he was!

The lady *gasped*, but then she smiled. She told Hello Kitty that a family had reported a missing puppy just half an hour ago — it must be the same one! She would go and have an announcement put out over the loudspeakers so the owners could come and find him.

Hello Kitty explained that she had **promised** Mama she would stay by the trees, so she wouldn't be able to come with her, and the lady nodded. It was very sensible of Hello Kitty not to go away from where her parents had left her! She said that she would take the puppy with her to the announcement tent and reached out for him, but the puppy didn't want to go to her!

He kept cuddling down further and further into Hello Kitty's arms!

The lady **laughed.** Hello Kitty had obviously made a new friend. Maybe it would be best if she went to make the announcement without the puppy – would Hello Kitty be OK to wait there with him until she got back?

Hello Kitty nodded. That was fine with her! The lady hurried off. The puppy *squirmed* in Hello Kitty's arms; he wanted to get down. She put him on the grass but held on to the lead tightly. He pulled her back to the plant pots and started sniffing and pawing at them. Hello Kitty crouched down beside him. *One, two* and UP!

The puppy climbed up and into one of the pots, his legs waving; he wriggled round and peered out over the top. Hello Kitty laughed. He looked adorable with his head popping out – all that you could see were his little nose, ears and mouth. Gently, Hello Kitty helped him out and began playing with the pots with him. They had a lovely time together. After a while,

Mama White came to check on Hello Kitty.

She was very surprised to see the puppy but

pleased with Hello

Kitty for having done

the right thing by

staying where she

was and telling

an official. She sat

down and played with

the puppy, too, and he

showed off his trick of climbing into the

plant pot.

Mama White **chuckled.** He really did

look very cute!

Fifteen minutes later, the festival helper and a little boy and another lady came hurrying over to the tree. They must be his owners! They bent down to pick him and gave him a hug as the little puppy's tail wagged furiously. The boy and his mother had been so worried about

the missing puppy! They thanked Hello Kitty for taking care of him and told her that his name was Basil. For one awful moment they thought that they had lost him

forever – but here he was, safe and sound!

Hello Kitty gave Basil one last pat and said

that it had been no trouble at all looking after

him. She always liked making new friends –

whether they were human or animal! Everyone

smiled at each other and the boy hugged

the puppy tightly.

As they turned to go, Mama White checked her watch. Oh dear… they had lost track of time… They had better go and find Mimmy and Papa straightaway. The baking workshop was about to **start!**

Bake Off Time!

Mama and Hello Kitty hurried across the park, weaving in and out of all the people. Hello Kitty realised she still hadn't thought of a cake... but at least she'd helped Basil find his family. That was far more important! They reached the **big**

tent to find the rest of the Friendship Club
already there, as well as Mimmy and Papa. The
parents all helped the
children sign in for
the competition
and said that
they would
come back at
four o'clock to
collect them, just in
time for the picnic.

As they *waved* goodbye to their parents
and headed into the tent, Hello Kitty told her
friends all about Basil. They thought it sounded

very exciting and that the puppy sounded really cute. If **only** they'd been able to meet him too!

There were two people running the workshop – Molly and James – who handed out white aprons and big chef hats for them all to put on.

Soon, everyone was making sandwiches with freshly baked bread, perfect **puffy** sausage rolls, mini quiches and yummy scones, along with **big** jugs of fruit punch – everything for the perfect picnic.

At last it was time to make their cakes. Molly and James asked what everyone was going to do – they **nodded** at people for them to call out their ideas. One girl announced that she was going to make a **robot** cake, and another put in that she would be making chocolate cornflake cakes! Molly explained that all of the basic ingredients would be there for them, but they should have brought the finishing touches to decorate them from home. Everyone nodded; they all knew

that. Dear Daniel produced
his liquorice and fruit drops,
and Fifi got out some cute
little model skaters to put
on her cupcakes. Tammy had
crafted a *cute* yellow bookworm at
home out of pom-poms and pipe cleaners, ready
to pop on the top of her book-shaped cake. But
Hello Kitty didn't have any special ingredients!

She would just be making
her white chocolate and
raspberry cake, although
maybe she could do it in
one of the different shaped

tins there or decorate it in some way to make it stand out…

Suddenly, a light bulb went off in Hello Kitty's head. She might have THOUGHT she didn't have an idea, but one had actually **popped** into her head just

that very second! It was to do with the puppy and the flowerpots. Perhaps she didn't need any special ingredients after all – instead of baking her cake in a boring round cake tin like usual, she could split

the mix up and bake it in the three flowerpots!

The cakes would *rise* while they were cooking

and then she could decorate the rounded tops

by making the eyes and nose and ears out of

icing. If her idea worked, the cakes would look

like they were puppies peering out of the pots!

Hello Kitty hurried over to explain her idea to Molly and James. She asked them if it would be safe to put the pots in the oven and they said that they didn't see why not… If the clay of the pots was terracotta, they would be oven-proof and a lovely, **fresh** way to present a cake! If she had the pots, then they had all the ingredients that she

would need to ice them.

Hello Kitty took the flowerpots over to the

sink to give them a good wash and a *scrub*, as

everyone set to work. Soon the tent was a hive

of activity with everyone measuring and stirring

and sifting and pouring. All of the cakes went

into the ovens and then all the bakers *helped*

to clear up!

They tidied and put away, and just as they

finished the washing up, the cakes were ready to take out of the oven. Once they had **cooled**, they were ready to ice, and thirty minutes later the class stood back to admire their work.

Hello Kitty *and friends*

The Friendship Club had done brilliantly. They

had all had such different ideas but their cakes

all looked really SUPER!

Dear Daniel's spider

was a bit **messy,**

but the thick

chocolate icing looked

delicious. Fifi's ice-skating cupcakes

looked very *pretty* with the ice-skaters on top

and Tammy's sponge bookworm

cake was admired as a real

work of art. Tammy had

even written the book

title on the cover and

the bookworm was very cute! Hello Kitty

congratulated

all her friends

and then

looked at her

own flowerpot

cakes. She was

very pleased. They had

turned out just as she hoped and they

seemed to make everyone

smile. They

especially made HER

smile because they

reminded her of a

very special puppy!

There was just one question left now – who was going to win?

Star Bakers!

The picnic rugs were spread out, the places were set and little fairy lights lit up the inside of the big tent. The picnic was ready to begin! Molly and James brought out the platters of food. The Friendship Club were joined by their parents and

they all started to fill their plates. There were so many treats and lovely things to eat! As well as the sandwiches, rolls and quiches that the bakers had made, Molly and James were putting pizzas in a clay oven. How would they ever get through it all? James told Hello Kitty and her friends that if any food was left over, it could be taken home to eat.

Mama White was still talking excitedly about the different cheeses she had tried when they sat down. Hello Kitty wasn't sure who had had *more* fun – her mother or Papa White, who couldn't stop talking about his cider pressing! But at last a contented silence filled the tent and everyone started munching on their food.

Hello Kitty was surprised when they were finished and only a few crumbs were left on the plates – she had felt sure that they'd never be able to eat it all, but James explained that it happened every year – they always said that if there was anything left over it could be taken home, but there never was!

And now, since everyone had finished eating, Molly and James moved to the front of the tent — it was time for the winner of the most original cake to be **announced!**

Everyone in the tent hushed as Molly stood up to make her speech. She announced in a loud voice that all those who had taken part were all Star Bakers in her eyes and that everyone would be getting a signed certificate for that…

but in third place, a girl with strawberry-blonde hair and a face full of freckles was called up for her robot cake! As everyone **clapped,** the girl grinned and went up to collect her ribbon. In second place... Everyone in the tent **hushed** again... It was Tammy for her bookworm cake! Hooray!

The Friendship Club

let out a loud

cheer

as Tammy

stood and

took her

ribbon. And

then, in first

place… Molly was

silent for a few moments before she started to

speak. In first place was…

HELLO KITTY! Her flowerpot cakes had been

a hit with everyone – they had not only looked

very cute – they had tasted amazing too!

The Friendship Club gave Hello Kitty an extra loud **cheer** as she blushed and went up to get her shiny silver cup. Hello Kitty didn't think she could have felt prouder as she held it in her hands and everybody **clapped**. She was presented with a red ribbon as well that she pinned to her chest. Who would have thought it? Just that morning she still hadn't even had an idea of what she was going to bake. If she hadn't bumped into that puppy she'd never had known…

The **puppy!**

At that moment, a loud shout rang

out around the tent. Everyone looked up as a woman and a boy raced in, chasing a little brown flash of colour that was racing towards the front. It was Basil! The little sausage dog threw himself at Hello Kitty and gave her a *massive* lick.

Hello Kitty smiled and gave him an extra **big** hug.

Basil's lead was trailing behind him, so Hello Kitty made a grab for it and handed it back to the little boy. He **smiled** and thanked her, and his Mama said she was glad that Basil had made such a good friend – even if they were going to have to do a lot of work with puppy training if they were going to get him under control! Everyone laughed and Hello Kitty giggled and smiled. It was always good to make new friends.

Hello Kitty felt a little fizz of happiness flood

through her. It had been

a brilliant day! A day full of fun and adventure.

And, she thought, it called for a brand new

Friendship Club motto:

New friends are like good ideas – sometimes they turn up when you least expect them!

She couldn't wait to tell her friends.

But the day wasn't over yet... There was

still the rest of the food festival to look round and they definitely needed to have a go on the bouncy castle. Hello Kitty looked around at her friends and grinned. It was time to go and play – SUPER!

The end

Turn over the page for activities and fun
things that you can do with your friends
– just like Hello Kitty!

Hello Kitty's
Best friend Biscuits

Hello Kitty loves baking biscuits for her friends. Hello Kitty makes hers heart-shaped, but circles, stars or flowers would be perfect too! Use your imagination to decorate each biscuit differently for each of your friends.

Let's get baking!

You will need:

Scales and measuring spoons

A baking tray

A wooden spoon

A biscuit cutter

A whisk

A large mixing bowl

rolling pin

A small bowl

A wire rack

For about 20 biscuits:
100g softened butter
100g caster sugar
1 medium egg
275g plain flour
2 teaspoons vanilla extract

For the decorations:
Tubes of coloured icing
Rainbow sprinkles

What to do!

1. Ask your grown-up helper to turn on the oven to 190°C (370°F / gas mark 5).

190°C

2.

Cut out a piece of greaseproof paper the same size as your baking tray and use a little butter to stick it down.

3.

Mix the butter and sugar together in the large bowl, stirring hard until the mixture is light and fluffy.

4. Break the egg into the small bowl, add the vanilla extract and whisk gently.

5.

Add the egg and vanilla to the butter and sugar mixture a little at a time, stirring well as you go.

6.

Stir in the flour until the mixture starts to come together to make a dough. Use your hands if it gets too stiff to stir. Make sure they are clean first!

7.

Sprinkle a little extra flour on to your work surface and roll out the dough with the rolling pin until it is about 1cm thick.

8.

Cut out biscuit shapes using your biscuit cutter and arrange them on the baking tray.

9.

Ask your grown-up helper to put the tray in the oven, and leave it for 8-10 minutes until your biscuits are pale and golden.

8-10

10.

Ask your grown-up helper to take your biscuits out of the oven and lay them out on a wire rack to cool.

11.

When your biscuits are cool, decorate them for your friends. First write each name with icing, then add pretty icing patterns and shake rainbow sprinkles on top.

12.

It's time to give your friends their biscuits – what a scrummy surprise!

Crazy Cakes!

Hello Kitty and her friends had such super cake ideas. Here are their cakes and some others you could try making.

Dear Daniel's Spider Cake

Make a round chocolate sponge cake and ice it with gooey chocolate icing. Use liquorice for the legs and orange and green jelly drops for the feet and eyes to make it super spooky!

Tammy's bookworm cake

Make a rectangular sponge cake
and ice it with ready-to-roll icing
coloured with food colouring.
Make the cute bookworm
by threading little pompoms
together.

Rocking robot cake

Use a square sponge cake for the
robot's body, a smaller one for its
head and mini Swiss rolls for legs
and arms. Cover with icing and
have fun adding sweets for the
robot's eyes, mouth and controls.

Hello Kitty Cake

Use two round sponge cakes to cut out a Hello Kitty face shape. Cover with white icing and use liquorice for her whiskers, nose and eyes. Ready-to-roll icing coloured pink makes her pretty bow. Perfect!

Turn the page for a sneak peek at

and friends'

next adventure...

Winter Wonderland

Hello Kitty looked out of the window of her sitting room. Perfect white snowflakes were flurrying down, settling on the garden. She felt a shiver of excitement fizzle through her. There was just one week left till Christmas and already it had started to snow! How SUPER was that!

Not so super, though, was her broken leg,

which was propped up on a cushion in front of her. It had been in a cast now for four weeks – ever since she had landed badly in a gymnastics competition and broken it. Hello Kitty let out a little sigh. Still, at least meant she had the chance to make Christmas cards for Dear Daniel, Tammy and Fifi. Hello Kitty smiled as she thought about her friends – her very best friends in the whole world. Together they made up the Friendship Club – a club that met after school and in the holidays to do all sorts of fun things like baking and painting and visiting fun places!

Today the rest of the Friendship Club were out ice-skating. Hello Kitty couldn't go because of her broken leg but her friends had promised to call in afterwards. She checked the clock; she really should get on with their cards...

Find out what happens next in...

Hello Kitty's Secret Word

Unscramble the letters and
solve the puzzle to discover
Hello Kitty's secret word.

A sweet, juicy fruit
S E T B R R Y A R W
☐ ☐ ☐ ☐ ☐ ☐ ☐ ☐ ☐

The lost puppy's name was...
B S L A I
☐ ☐ ☐ ☐ ☐

Hello Kitty and her friends made...
K E S A C
☐ ☐ ☐ ☐ ☐

The family all went to a food...
L V T S E I F A
☐ ☐ ☐ ☐ ☐ ☐ ☐ ☐

The Secret Word is:
☐ ☐ ☐ ☐

Go to **www.harpercollins.co.uk/HelloKittyandFriends**
Enter the secret word to download your exclusive
Hello Kitty activities, games and fun!